WHO MADE THE MORNING?

For my mother, Mary Ribbons

WHO MADE THE MORNING?

Jan Godfrey

Illustrated by Jane Cope

VICTOR BOOKS

A DIVISION OF SCRIPTURE PRESS PUBLICATIONS INC.
USA CANADA ENGLAND

Once upon a time there was a Little Brown Bird who lived at the top of a tall, tall tree.

One beautiful morning Little Brown Bird bounced out of her nest. She bounced so much that she rocked the tree and woke up all the other birds. They just yawned and grumbled.

It was the most wonderful morning that Little Brown Bird had ever seen.

Little Brown Bird fluttered about happily. "Who made this beautiful morning?" she said to herself.

She thought she would ask the flowers.

"Flowers, can you tell me something? Who made this beautiful morning?"

But the flowers turned their petals away from her toward the sun.

"I know," thought Little Brown Bird, "I'll ask the cow."
"Cow," began Little Brown Bird, "do you know who. . . ."
"MOO! WHO?!" mooed the cow. She mooed so loudly
that Little Brown Bird was frightened and flew away to a
quiet corner of her tree.

The other birds were sitting in a row on a branch, wide awake now, and chattering happily.

"Birds, can you tell me who made this beautiful morning?" asked Little Brown Bird.

"Don't know, don't care," said the chattering birds, and they all giggled and laughed and rolled about.

"Perhaps I could ask the clouds," she thought.
"Clouds, do you know who made this beautiful morning?"
The clouds were in a hurry but the little breeze blowing
them across the sky whispered very softly, "God the Maker
of all the World made this beautiful morning."

"Oh! Thank you," said Little Brown Bird. "Thank you,
Breeze, for telling me. But who is He? Where does He live?"
But the breeze left Little Brown Bird alone with the
beautiful morning.

15

"I shall fly and fly until I find out where God the Maker of all the World lives," Little Brown Bird sang out to all the other birds. "Then I can tell Him how much I like this beautiful morning."

Little Brown Bird flew over the countryside. Then she flew over a busy town with cars and trains and buses.

She flew on higher over the silver, sparkling river, and the blue, shimmering lake.

It was getting colder now. Little Brown Bird flew toward the snowy mountain tops, higher than she had ever flown before. And then . . .

Suddenly the black shadow of an eagle
filled the sky.

Little Brown Bird was frightened. She
darted this way and that to escape the
fierce eyes and curved beak.

"Please help me! Somebody help me,"
she cried.

Just at that moment, the eagle turned and flew away.

By now the sky had gone dark. Cold starry snowflakes whirled past Little Brown Bird. The wind blew so hard it blew her on to a rocky ledge.

She was cold and hungry.

She was lost.

She was tired.

Little Brown Bird lay down on the rock and went to sleep.

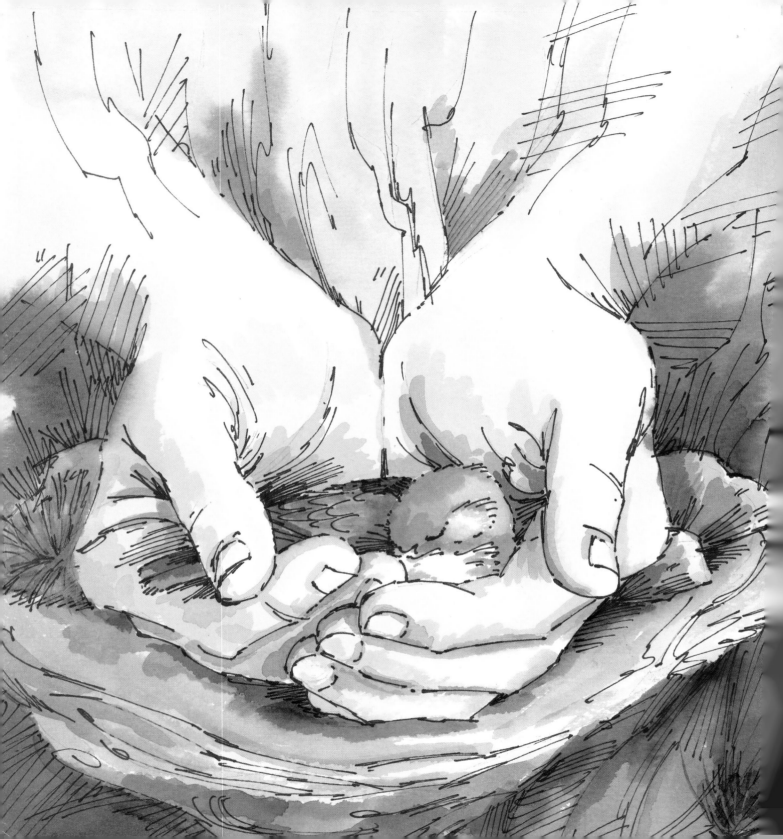

While Little Brown Bird was asleep,
she dreamed that God the Maker of all the
World was holding her ever so carefully in
His hands.
   She felt happy.
   She felt safe.

When she woke up, the morning sun was warm. The eagle and the storm had gone and she wasn't cold and tired any more. But she was hungry.

A gentle breeze lifted her up into the air and she knew she would be able to find her way home.

She crossed the lake and the river and she flew over the town. She flew back over the fields and trees and bushes. She was nearly home . . .

And then Little Brown Bird understood something wonderful, something so wonderful that she knew she would always remember it. "God the Maker of all the World is with me all the time, wherever I go," she thought.

"Did you find God the Maker of all the World?" asked the chattering birds.

"Yes," said Little Brown Bird happily. "But He doesn't live in just one place. He was with me in all the places I went and He looked after me."

"What is he like?" asked the chattering birds.

"He's stronger than the wind, and He's brighter than the sun," said Little Brown Bird. "He's greater than the eagle and the storm, and He has brought me home."

Then Little Brown Bird hopped up and down and said, "And God the Maker of all the World made this beautiful morning!"

And she sang a happy song.

"Look at the birds! They don't worry about what to eat—
they don't need to sow or reap or store up food—for
Your heavenly Father feeds them. And you are far more
valuable to him than they are."

(Matthew 6:26)

A Tamarind Book

1995 edition published by Victor Book/SP Publications, Inc.

in association with SU Publishing

130 City Road, London EC1V 2NJ